SPEEDY SPIDERS

AMAZING

TECHNI
COLOURED
WEB

Spider climbed and climbed till he reached the top as he looked down he mapped his course.

Wheeeee, as he bungeed off the side, till he reached the bottom.

Climbing as fast as he could he jumped again.

Wheeeeee, till he reached the bottom again.

Up and down, up and down, till he went right around.

Then Speedy worked his web, in and out, in and out,

till he went right around.

Feeling pleased with himself, Speedy Spider hid in the corner waiting for his lunch.

A small fly, a moth, maybe if he's lucky a big daddy longlegs,

as he licks his lips dreaming of his lunch.

Spider waited and waited, until his eyes started to close,

Deep in sleep he dreamt till the sun came up.

Then... woosh ! The water shot up, scaring speedy spider as he cowered in the web.

Slowly spider looked around to see his web was still intact. He sat and stared, quite mesmerised at the water fountain.

As people gathered, they pointed at the funny colours coming from behind the water fountain,

Blues, greens, reds and yellows, gold and silver, shimmering off his web, when the light hit through the cascade of water.

As the day went on the lights came on inside the water fountain.

Spiders web shone out through the spray, changing colours as the crowd went ooooooooooooh, aaaaaaaaaaaaaah.

Suddenly speedy Spider had an idea, as he shot around his web changing the shape's.

A kaleidoscope of colours changing every time speedy went around.

First there was squares changing into triangles then he sped around again doing hexagons finally finishing with the most difficult circles.

As the crowd grew, the colours glistened off the webs making everyone watching make a wish, throwing a penny in the fountain.

As the night went on the water stopped, letting in some mesmerized flies for spiders supper.

Gobbling them down, he went to sleep.

Only to wake up as his web had been washed away.

Speedy spider started again, up and down, up and down, and all around, just in time before the water shot out.

As the lights went on, a crowd gathered again watching speedy spider's web change colours and shapes.

Around and around he spun all night, wowing the crowd till the water went out.

The well was full of pennies, and the web was full of supper as the spider filled his belly.

Fast asleep Speedy snored, as his web got washed away.

Speedy woke with a stretch and a yawn before racing up and down and all around making his web, before the water shot out again.

As word got around speedy spider had an audience of people all Around

OOOOOOOh,

AAAAAAAAAh from all around as speedy sped around changing the shapes as all the different colours shone out,

All summer he worked hard wowing the crowd till it got too cold for speedy spider to carry on.

See you next summer, he wrote out.

THE END

Printed in Great Britain
by Amazon